Gallery Books
Editor: Peter Fallon

OVEN LANE

Michael Coady

OVEN LANE

Gallery Books

Oven Lane
is first published
simultaneously in paperback
and in a clothbound edition
on 17 December 1987.

The Gallery Press
19 Oakdown Road
Dublin 14, Ireland

© Michael Coady 1987

ISBN 1 85235 020 2 (*paperback*)
   1 85235 021 0 (*clothbound*)

The Gallery Press receives financial assistance from An Chomhairle
Ealaíon / The Arts Council, Ireland.

Contents

Acknowledgements

Acknowledgements are due to the editors of *Cyphers*, *Dal gCais*, *Fortnight*, *The Honest Ulsterman*, *The Irish Times*, *Krino*, *The Nationalist* (Clonmel), *The Irish Press* (New Irish Writing), *Poetry Ireland Review*, *Poets for Africa*, *Poets Live*, *Riverine*, *Rostrum*, R.T.E. and *The Salmon* in which some of these poems were published first.

In the writing of this book the author acknowledges the support of An Chomhairle Ealaíon / The Arts Council, Ireland, through a bursary and, toward the book's completion, a stay at the Tyrone Guthrie Centre, Annaghmakerrig.

The word is also flesh, and simple bread
is happiness and mystery.

– Osip Mandelstam

for my mother and father

Letting Go

I love the abandon
of abandoned things

the harmonium surrendering
in a churchyard in Aherlow,
the hearse resigned to nettles
behind a pub in Carna,
the tin dancehall possessed
by convolvulus in Kerry,
the living room that hosts
a tree in south Kilkenny.

I sense a rapture
in deserted things

washed-out circus posters
derelict on gables,
lush forgotten sidings
of country railway stations,
bat droppings profligate
on pew and font and lectern,
the wedding dress a dog
has nosed from a dustbin.

I love the openness
of things no longer viable,
I sense their shameless
slow unbuttoning:
the implicit nakedness
there for the taking,
the surrender to the dance
of breaking and creating.

The Fruit

Behind the rouge grotesquely daubed
on brittle cheekbones, yellowed skin,
is ash upon the brow of her forefathers

stiff in ledgered certainties
scripted in the hedge school
of suppurating fields –

a yard of counter
is better than
an acre of ground.

Under this day's glorias and glad tidings
recall a frail birth-cry
lost Christmases ago

above a shop tight-shuttered
against sun and rain
and whisper at the window

where an only girl was bound
in swaddling clothes of grey
respectability that feared

the unaccountable, the hazarding
of heart which is life's seed
and spendthrift ground,

that weighed out parloured
caution which would shape at last
this piteous flesh and bone

to kneel before
a plaster infant
on this day

a rouged memento mori whispering
blessèd is the fruit.

A Blue Gate in Lough Street

'I have no mockings or arguments, I witness and wait'
                                    – Walt Whitman

The seed,
the sun,
the days,
the leaf and birdsong,
the axe,
the saw and plane,
the hands,

the years
on layered years
of tar,
the blister and the scar
of weathers,

all topped in time
with this inspired
epiphany of blue,
the deep
dark blue
of spaces,
silences.

Behind it,
through the slow
turn of nights,
the ritual of hands
with yeast and flour,
with salt and water

and from the oven
time and time again
the incensed miracle

of bread, its truth
and grace, brought
out to light
and offered
to the morning.

All the while
the wood was earning
its adagio complexity

under the palette knife
of cold and heat,
of dark and wind and day,
of goings
and returnings.

Yes, all of it's timescaped
behind a child
who's playing hopscotch
on the footpath

who's dancing
between earth and air
against this scarred
epiphany of blue

the deep
dark blue
of spaces,
silences.

Commonwealth

How odd of my wife
I thought at the time
to pluck bay leaves
to season her stews
from a tree that shades
the grave of a girl
in Kilclispeen.

Mary Dempsey
knew seventeen springs
before they laid her
into the earth,
before the bay tree
put down roots

before my mother
and father knew
fruit of the tree
of life.

Sitting at table
with wife and child
I relish the dish
and acknowledge the guest
who is part of the feast –

you're welcome, Mary,
into my house
and you're more than welcome
into my mouth

for this is the way
the world goes round
from the first kiss

to the baby's milk,
from the first word
to the tongue's last sound –

bread of communion
we taste in the mouth
is broken in commonwealth
under the ground.

Tracing a Cracked High B Flat for Posterity

– there's the wallflowered shell
of the Wadding Charity 1756
where my great great grandfather
the boatman Jimmy Coady of Hayes's Lane
died in 1895 attended only by his
grandson Michael who'd been raised
as an orphan after his father
skipped around 1880 to marry again
with a woman named Brunnock in
Philadelphia where they were lost to view

while the child my grandfather Michael became
a skilled solicitor's clerk, played billiards,
the fiddle, and drank, once threw a Christmas
pudding into the fire when my grandmother
a hard woman of the Victorian
shopkeeper class had taken the hatchet to
his irresponsible fiddle once and for all
or so she believed in her Beecham's pills
and the strength of her corseted rosaries

at his death of t.b. in 1932 the Brass Band
sober in black slow marched the large and
representative attendance including afflicted
widow across the Old Bridge 1447 to the
dead march from Saul and with cases of
stout in the offing for the gaslit years
of nights he'd conducted them through
Pinafore, *Maritana* and *Poet and Peasant*
never having forgiven his son my father George
for a cracked high B flat in the solo euphonium
cadenza at the great Band Contest Wexford 1925

so that all his life that cracked high B flat
haunted my father until his death not quite

sober in 1973 just as he'd sung there's a long
trail a-winding into the land of my dreams
at which stage I was a man of sorts sidling
towards marriage and having my own troubles
with high B flat on the trombone, something
to do with the shape of the family mouth

not to mention an old woman, ninety-three but
not telling, who smiles at me every Sunday,
who long ago played the piano, especially duets with
my grandfather Michael and I've heard their
long ago music put the Christmas pudding
into the fire and the fiddle in smithereens
I'd love to ask her straight out before
she dies if it's true she had a musical
fling with my grandfather seventy years ago
but of course she's a lady and won't ever tell

that's me now standing outside the butcher's
at the top of New Street, glasses and developing
paunch, at half past four in May 1983
high on the wallflowered shell
of the Wadding Charity 1756 where
my great great grandfather died in 1895
just up the street from the Town Hall
where every Tuesday night I conduct
the Brass Band with tolerance and even
love for cracked high B flats

at the moment half past four in May 1983
I'm still above ground and feel okay and
I mean to be drunk tonight for unstoppable
wallflowers not to mention my wife who is
pregnant and much else besides such as
that man at the corner who can unblock

the drains dig the graves put out fires
arrest stray dogs or sing like Slim Whitman
or the way that the girl who works
in the bookie's moves as she walks
across the street and into the butcher's
behind me or the shape of the consequential
clouds at this moment over my head –

Naming Names

Dead Bell
Lousy Town
Black Ink
Foot of Ebb

Flash Colours
Make it the Two
Long Distance
Cursèd Good-Lookin'

Hard Lines
Stand Back
Cracked Eggs
Hand on Flap

Cat Out
Belly o' Pups
Dead Man
Top o' the Pot

Wobbler
Feathery
Tom the Bard

Axle
Ginchy
Bucket o' Blood

Hambone
Hawkeye
Live Wire

Sugar
Goitre
Stab the Rasher

Barrel
Oblong
Slobbery Gob

Incarnation

Today is the feast of the body,
the body of Christ,
the blossoming body
of everything

and summer is carried
through the streets
under a golden canopy
with incense and rose petals
by Canon Delaney sprung
out of farmland
over the mountain

with shuffle and sway of the people
making a deep-toned mantra
of *blessèd* and *fruit* and *womb*
through Town Wall and West Gate,
Main Street and New Street

passing by a table whitespread
under lilies and Sacred Heart
in the flowering doorway
of Mary Hanrahan's *Takeaway*,
by the face of Perpetual Succour
in the window of Meany's Shoes,

by Martha Callaghan's pink Salon
where passé models in permanent waves
have surrendered to candles
and Infant of Prague,

by the Comeragh Bar where the Virgin
is vested in freshcut roses,
by the Bank of Ireland rich
in the flag of the Pope.

The summer is carried
past garage and lane and drapery store
with trombones and cornets and bass drum,
with cymbals and horns and euphonium
brassing the heavy air

with mortal voices choiring
Sweet Sacrament divine
Hid in Thine earthly home

tenor and bass and soprano
telling the street and the river and sky
With suppliant hearts we come.

In the Town Park and under the trees
Canon Delaney sprung
out of farmland
over the mountain
offers a sacrifice

raises the Host
to the tinkle of bell
in the incensed evening

and holds in the chalice
the trees and the grass and the people,
the children and dogs and the birdsong,
the band and the leaves and the clouds.

He breaks in his fingers
Corpus Christi,
the day and the summer
and blossoming body:

people move forward
to eat of it
before the long dusk
comes down.

Terminal Talk

His mouth has shifted sideways, a binding
bears his chin up, covers one ear
and the mad rampaging stranger
his neck and jaw are host to.
Though the sounds are mutilated
he can't stop talking. He is past
all camouflage of smalltalk,
all time for courtesies.

Everything I try to say
stinks of evasion; my mouth is
a crippled mechanical thing
discharging cliché, sucking
at straws of chat to kill the hour.
I see that he is angry because
I fail to meet his naked words
with nakedness, because my mouth
pretends he lies alone.

Living dangerously
he says what he likes –
last night he took a young nun's hand,
told her she should have children,
take a man, and damn
the vow of chastity to hell.
Now he tells me not to visit him again
if all I have to say is shit
about the traffic and the weather.

I grasp his hand
before I say goodnight, evading
the terrible candour of his eyes,
sweating for the anodyne
of mundane air, the easy
valium of the commonplace.

The Letter

for James Coady, lost father of my grandfather

1.
If there can be some
redemption in the word
then let this telling reach
across the silence
of a hundred years
in Oven Lane.

About your feet upon the earthen floor
let me find the child who will
out of the slow unravelling
become my grandfather
and in the curtained room
your young wife Mary Eager
still beside an infant
bound with her in rituals
of laying-out and prayer.

This dark hour's nativity
will shape and scar your destiny
and in the unformed future
cast its shadow over hearts
that will engender me;
in time it will call up
this impulse
and these words.

Let me try to know you
in the anguish of that hour

a man of no importance
trapped in a narrow place,
enmeshed in desperate circumstance

as at the whim of some
malignant puppeteer.

The image holds the lane,
its stench, the fetid hovels
crowding down toward
the quayside of the Suir
where kinship and compassion
resurrect in time upon the page
the murmured solidarity
and flickering of candles
about the human face
of piteous travail.

2.
A hundred years and I will come
to try the lane for echoes

the coughing and the crying
of children in the dark,
the nameless incarnations
of love and grief and hunger
where the river flows
coldly past.

These broken walls were witness
to your leaving, whether
in morning sun or rain,
your firstborn child still sleeping
when you left him,
the dark-shawled blessings
from the doorways of a lane
you'd never see again.

3.

What I know has come to me
out of dead mouths:
through the barefoot child
left with your father,
the old boatman, and from
the mouth of my own father,
that child's son.

A life I'll never know
is buried with you
in a place
I'll never find:

a generation turned before
the morning of the letter
sent to find your son
become a man
with children of his own.

Out of the maze of circumstance,
the ravelled tangle of effect and cause,
something impelled you,
brought you finally
to bend above
the unmarked page –

an old man
in some room in Philadelphia
reaching for words to bridge
the ocean of his silence,
pleading forgiveness of the child
of Oven Lane.

4.
Silence was the bitter
answer you were given
every empty day
until you died:

by a breakfast table
my child father
watched your son unseal
his darkest pain

saw the pages torn and cast
in mortal grief and anger
out of an abandoned child's
unspeakable heart-hunger
into the brute finality
of flame.

5.
Now all of these
have gone into the dark
and I would try again
to reconcile the hearts
of which my heart's compounded
with words upon a page.

I send this telling out
to meet the ghosts
of its begetting,
to release it from stone mouths
of Oven Lane.

Newborn Feet

Toward what rooms,
what doors and windows
will those unshod feet bear you?
There are things preparing –

there are others, born
or to be made, and they
will come to meet you
in the mystery of faring

toward unknown destinations
found by choice and chance
along unfolding paths
of questing and creating.

Video

They tell me that I am that stranger
at the head of the ragtaggle band
shuffling in step down Greystone Street
to the pulse of *The Young Recruit* –

that oddly intimate stranger
who is leading and led
in his grandfather's footsteps
and to the same harmonies

with Nick the Bard underlining
the ballast of time on the drum,
inciting the tatty bravura
of a distant imperium.

As the face blurs close to the lens
I search the grain
for another –

I look myself in the face
through eyes which would
cut and run

to chance every morning's air
and burn on a nightly batter
of scandalous song.

Salmon Solstice

The salmon on the Town Clock
swims the air of every day
above our heads, above our lives.

Through each season's passing
lift your head
and raise your eyes

for in your mortal share
of breath and space and time
you may be granted blessing

of an instant when your eye,
the eye of salmon, and the light
align in mystical surprise

and with that sudden focus
all the great sun melts in magic,
sheds its gold upon you, flooding

through the eyehole of the salmon
spawned in fire and argument
bronze and hammer-stroke

at Foley's forge
by Clareen Well
one hundred years ago.

Sally Edmonds

1744-1747

All of human anguish
    is told upon this stone,
sorrow's tale is chiselled
    down to barest bone

did water fire or fever take
    this three year child away?
Little Sally Edmonds
    is two hundred years in clay.

Love that sparked her making
    in darkness of the past
whispered on white pillows
    or smiled in summer grass

hairs on head are numbered
    and sparrows count they say,
little Sally Edmonds
    is two hundred years in clay.

Facing the Music

It must be night he supposed
green in the glow from the monitors
of the hearts alive on the screens
in intensive care, with the man
in the next bed turning in sleep
and moaning a woman's name.

It must be night out there
with rain kissing the trees
beyond the dark glass of the window
and a girl in white above him
holding his hand and asking,
'are you feeling pain?'

I'm singing he thought or said,
I'm singing again with the band,
with the trumpets and saxes and rhythm,
with the pulse and sway of the crowd
to the night and the music.

Would you like to dance?
he said or he thought
to the girl in intensive care,
dim in the glow of the light
of the pulsing hearts in time,
knowing her shoulders under the dress
and her hair against his cheek –

I'm watching the green hearts dancing
holding a girl and singing,
moving in rhythm close to the river
that beats to the sea and the deep
of the dark, I'm feeling the pulse
of the band and I'm singing
Let's face the music and dance.

Stopping by a Clare Graveyard After Hours

for Pakie Russell, 1920-1977

I've walked up two miles from the pub
   through a mystical moonscape
And it could have been three what with taking
   both sides of the road,
I lean on the wall and my breathing
   is heavy and laboured
As I give you a greeting and offer you
   talk of the world.

Below in the village the men
   and the women are sleeping,
The lights are all out and the children
   away in their dreams,
The music and talk of tonight
   are gone to wherever
The tunes and the talk of all nights
   slip away on the air.

From shore to horizon the sea
   is a ravishing silver,
Awesome and innocent, untouched
   by joy or dismay;
The grass of the summer is gathered
   and tied in the haggards,
The dark brow of Moher is dreaming
   over the bay.

I'm not here to grieve for your bones
   or the earth where they're lying,
You've company round you of neighbours
   and friends from this place;
The men and the women who danced
   to your music are with you,

United you lie in the intimate
    rhythm of clay.

I know you were always a man
    with a heart for the true thing,
For a child or a saying, a woman,
    a flower or a song,
Life that came dancing through fingers
    was most of your praying
And your darkness redeemed in the shape
    and surprise of the word.

Out of all of the years and the laughter
    just let me remember
One moment of kissing I stood
    by the sea with a girl
While you were enthroned on the hill
    with the dawn at your shoulder
Gracing your music with wakening
    song of the birds.

The tiding old sea is still taking
    and giving and shaping,
Gentians and violets break
    in the spring from the stone,
The world and its mother go reeling
    and jigging forever
In answer to something that troubles
    the blood and the bone.

So I have to report there's no end
    to the song and the story,
With enough music in it to send us all
    drunk on our way;

As I go to my sleep I ask
for a smile and a blessing:
'S a chara mo chléibh, bí meidhreach
is gáirsiúil id' chré.

The Invisible Hotel

Stand at the turn and see quite clearly
Kennedy's Hotel no longer there; hold
in the eye this void where everything
ordinary happened in its time

and slow-dissolved into a clarified
intrigue of space now absolutely innocent
of every brick and wall and window, with all
of maids and cattle-jobbers, drinkers and cardplayers,
shoes and sheets and knives and pots and basins,
plates and dinners and the creaking stair
recycled utterly to air.

Flesh out the inventory with snores and singing,
boiled potatoes and the aftersmell of cabbage,
copulation, defecation and death-rattle,
glint of glass and amber eye of whiskey,
melodeons and chamber pots and sides of bacon,
fires alight and rain against the windows,
steam and coins and candles and
the grey rewind of mornings after.

Pick a card from out the shuffled
and reshuffled deck
of darkened instances –

the starched cuffs of Francesco Marchetti
come to sell beads and prayer books
from a booth during the Parish Mission
taking lamb's liver with his tea and all
unguessing that after sermon and Benediction
he'll meet his force of destiny in Mary Browne
who's still demurely cutting calico
upstairs under gaslight in the drapery
of P. Bourke & Co., Main Street,

or from the voided clamour and the whispering
choose the gone-to-silence scales and trills
of beautiful Miss Olive Westwood warming up
with Maestro Albert Bowyer on pianoforte
to give her golden arias above a trance of faces
in the Town Hall for that night only,
while in the dark backyard Liz Callaghan
is tipping slops to pigs
that fatten for the winter.

There, as clear as day,
it all no longer is
from where you're passing
between Town Wall and Lough Street,
under the salmon on the Town Clock
turning in the wind to spawn
each day's conspiring weather.

Wave and Undertow

1.

An inland child, I can remember
the moment I first met
the giant scope of sea,
advancing on my first
communion feet.

Eyelids heavy with horizons
between cool sheets I listened
to the landing clock conspiring
in the rituals of dark, a ship
remotely booming in the harbour.

Above me in the lamplight
gentle fingers of my grandmother
sprinkling holy water on
my face, my whispered words
– *what makes the waves?*

She bent to kiss my forehead –

*Almighty God makes waves and men
and light and dark –*

and turned down the lamp.

2.
*The quality of mercy is not strained:
It droppeth as the gentle rain from heaven
Upon the place beneath.*

My childheart measured summers
in the haven of her ways –

shutters barred against the dark,
hiss of gaslight over ironing,
milk saucered out to kittens, hands
kneading dough on a scoured table, lips
that quoted Shakespeare like a prayer.

Beside her in the organ loft for Benediction
heady with incense I heard the chant
of the Divine Praises, knew the stop she chose
for *Adoremus in Aeternum*, felt the flooring
tremble with the final diapason.

3.
For fifty years the handmaid to this liturgy
of praising, she should have slipped away at last
in innocence and balm of blessed unction.
But when I was grown old enough to think
my eye might hold the measure
of wave and undertow

some evil thing was born beneath
her porcelain of skin. It swelled
to overwhelm her mind at last,
make her mouth a host to words
that no one could believe
she'd ever use,
and leave her drowning
in a place of locks and fears.

Lifelines

for Niamh

Daughter, your eyes
are clearer than mine:

you've asked me why the top
and bottom of my pint don't mix

and why we're dropping coins
into a model lifeboat.

I've said that heavy things
sink to the bottom, and there are

unexpected storms, lives to be
snatched out of the wind.

Later in the rain
you take my hand

lead me through
a tumult of dark trees.

I flare a match
and fumble with the key.

Your face and hair are wet,
your eyes are shining.

Abandoned Churchyard

Shattered is the stone
Above a girl made mad by
Unrequited love.

The Poppy in the Brain

– They shall be remembered forever.

1.
Chance preserved in someone's bric-à-brac
this fading studio dream
of a Home Counties beauty smiling
in soft focus with the legend
'Buy War Bonds and Feed the Guns'

under which indelibly
he'd pencilled all his innocence
before he met the shrapnel
and the wire

I hope you get this safe
im all rite and been treted well
you need not worry I have
good blankits and am warm.

2.
I don't know how next time
they'll feed you for it,
how they'll lace and flavour up
the same old bullshit –
but they'll find a way

they'll find a way

and though I'd like to feel
you kids are smarter now
and not for gulling, let me
not feed you bullshit of my own,
while knowing in my heart's dismay

you'll line up and obey,

oh yes you will you know,
you always do –

you'll line up and obey.

Job Wilks and the River

'. . . of the 56th Regiment, who died accidentally by drowning, at Carrick-on-Suir, 17th July 1868, in his 28th year.'

I feel that I know you, Job Wilks –

no imperial trooper swaggering
these servile Tipperary streets
before my grandfather drew breath,
but a country lad out of Hardy,
drunk on payday and pining for Wessex,
flirting with Carrick girls
in fetid laneways after dark,

out of step on parade to Sunday Service
with comrades who loved you enough
to raise out of soldiers' pay this stone
which would halt my feet among nettles
now that jackdaws are free in the chancel,
Communion plate lies deep
in the dark of a bank vault,
and spinster daughter of the last
rector, in a home for the aged,
whispers all night to an only brother
dead these forty years in Burma.

How commonplace, Job Wilks, how strange
that this should be where
it would end for you, twenty-eight
summers after the midwife washed you.
With that first immersion
you took your part
in the music of what happens,
and an Irish river was flowing
to meet you, make you
intimate clay of my town.

On a July day of imperial sun
did your deluged eyes find
vision of Wessex, as Suir water
sang in your brain?

I know the same river you knew, Job,
the same sky and hill and stone bridge:
I hope there were Carrick girls with tears
for a country lad out of Hardy,
drunk on payday and pining
for Wessex.

Primal Waltz

Deep in November it seems
a luminous thing
to have known
so simple a grace

a day in the summer
the sea took us in
to its belly and breast
and lifted us lightly together

lifted beside me your head
sleek as a seal's from the wave,
saltwater brimming our shoulders
under the light.

Open as children
we gave ourselves
to the primal
waltz of the world

spreading our limbs
in the balance and sway
of ocean and moon,
of earth and its sun

our lives and their gravities
laid for a time
with our clothes
behind us up on the land

and nothing beneath us
or pressing about us
but the absolute
pulse of sea

lifting us
woman and man
into the fluid dance
where all of the dreaming began.

New World

Lovers are commonplace as day, so why
should I feel moved by this chance
glimpse of an uncaring starstruck
pair in a Chicago street, islanded
within their pristine pool of joy,
tasting with their hands and eyes
that fugitive and fabled spring
of shy collusion and surprise?

Why should a traveller feel so blessed
against the grimy street's cacophony
and frantic push of money-chasing,
among the flintfaced cops, the joggers
and pulsating roller skaters,
among the strip show touts and cool
receptionists, the loud construction
workers and the lost bag ladies?

Within this maelstrom I'm relearning
that ecstasy and innocence persist
like untouched havens, though everywhere
and always stormed by circumstance and
reefed about with dangers. Far from home
I'm blessed to find that lovers, though
forever falling out of love and into
everyday, are always there, that is

somewhere, and always gazing, gazing
deep into unmapped horizons, their
lifted hearts like ships full-sailing
as if they'd just descried a virgin
island or a dazzling El Dorado, as if
in their sweet turn and time
they hugged exclusively
some whispered secret out of Eden.

Assumption Day in Connecticut

1.
During the Mass I remember
they've already been dancing
sets on this day
at St. Brigid's Well, Liscannor.

I think of when Aranmen dipped and stroked
nine miles of wave in to Clare
with slap and seethe of
saltwater under the cowhide,
creak of raw timber,
waltzing horizons

and then walked with their women
ten miles of rising ground
up by the cliffs to the Blessèd Well
to pray and dance and drink
a full night before they turned
mute faces west again.

2.
Father Comefrey is old,
silver hair above a face
weathered toward Indian.

He's learned to live
with unoriginal sin,
talks in a tired voice
of nuclear threat and abortion
and drugs, reminds us

there are such things
as innocence and fidelity,
speaks of Our Lady on this day

and quotes someone who likened Mary to

a tensile strength that
keeps our faith from snapping
between stretched tensions of
the world's polarities.

He pauses and stares around
to let it sink, nods silently
as if confirming to himself
no one is listening.

Hell, old man,
I'm passing through;
I heard what you said
and believe it
most of the time
of almost everybody's
lady.

3.
We sing a hymn to Mary
from the parish bulletin sponsored
by *Di Pietro Real Estate,*
Bess Eaton Donuts,
Paloma Hair Design
and *Mr. Steak* –

under Baptism News
we welcome baby
Elizabeth Anne Pingpank
into the Christian family.

The tired priest looks as if
the world's an old sour apple
well beyond anyone's sweetening

until he gives Communion
to a man carrying an infant,
then stops,
lets everything
wait

lays an old mottled hand
on the baby's head
and smiles

smiles suddenly and long
like day discovering
peaks and valleys,
streaming through forests,
flooding dark canyons,
silvering lake and river –

the whole god-
damned thing
realizing itself
all over again.

4.
I leave ten dollars for
the Organ Restoration Fund,
meet my kind agnostic host
who's parked outside
communing with Dow Jones.

Did I enjoy the service?

When he straightens the car
on the highway
I lob my innocent
Irish question

when did the last Indians
dance in Connecticut?

Dance
for themselves,
their gods,
the land,
the trees,
the sacred springs,
the waltzing horizons,
the tensile strength
of women?

He doesn't know;
he's working in insurance

but there's someone into
the ethnic thing
on the staff of Farmington High.

She might know something.

Thirsting

If you should ask me why
your mornings bring from me
no air mailed intimacies
I'd argue that the heart
of love is shy of saying,
its miraculous surprise
sings best in contained silence,
speaks truest when it's dumb,
free of the word's daylit
finalities, its bleary grime
of usage.

In a Greyhound terminal
the burnt out phrase which I
don't launch upon the air
is weak as tepid water
from this drinking fountain,
giving itself indifferently
to every traveller's mouth.

Better the sustenance of thirst
which contemplates the sharp
inviolate delight of untouched
springs, savours a parched
long-distance argument
for singing dumb.

Assembling the Parts

Standing in sunshine
by Highway 84
I'm photographing a factory
which is no longer there

looking for my father
by an assembly line
which has halted
and vanished into air

catching the sepia ghost
of a young tubercular Irishman
who's left a rooming house
at 6 a.m. in a winter time
during the Depression

when my mother is still a girl
playing precocious violin,
a Miraculous Medal under
her blouse, in Protestant
oratorios in Waterford.

A pallid face in the crowd
in a dark winter time,
he's coughing in the cold,
assembling typewriters
in Hartford, Connecticut,

waiting for blood on his pillow
to send him home, where he'll
meet her one ordinary
night with the band playing
Solitude in the Foresters' Hall.

Fifty years on
he's nine Septembers dead
and a tourist in sunshine
by Highway 84
is photographing a factory
which is no longer there,

assembling the parts
of the mundane mystery,
the common enigma of journeys
and unscheduled destinations,

the lost intersections
of person and place and time
uniquely fathering everyman
out of the random dark.

The Pursuit of Happiness

1.
I think of that amazing phrase
from the Founding Fathers
when cousin Steve brakes at the intersection
to let two girls in shorts cross over
to *Plaisir d'Amour* boutique

> *– I tell ya Mike*
> *there's ass*
> *there's good ass*
> *and there's great ass*
> *but there's no such thing*
> *as a bad piece of ass.*
> *Right?*

Cousin Steve is fifty and good natured.
He wears red tartan golfing trousers,
sells roofing tiles over the 'phone
and lives between his mother Leah
and Lorraine, long-legged widow of a trumpet player
who hit too many high notes
too often in his time.

Steve's driving me around to see
Easthampton's *pretty homes.*
I'm here ten years too late to meet
his father, the brother of my own.

2.
Near Montauk Point I plunge
deep under waves. A great swell
lifts me up into the sunshine,
shows me, for a moment to the east,
Ocean, and all the weight of exile.

Above the point a small plane
trails a banner through the blue:
Lobster Dinners at The Red Fox: $11.75

Beers at *The Patio*, in the corner where
my uncle spent his years of evenings;
nights he bored the barman with retelling
of celestial voices he once heard
before the breadlines and the crash of '29
when he was young, and standing
for three dollars at the Met.,
transfixed by Gigli and Ponselle
in *La Forza del Destino*.

Impassioned voices haunted all that life
of days he lettered village signs
when there was work, and watched
as year by year the New York rich
bought up the foreshore
for their summer homes.

3.
Leah, his widow, is almost eighty
but still has style. She jokes
about her bones and drives her beat-up
Chevy better than she walks.
Now, through the nights alone
she leans on vodka and on valium
that she hides when Steve's at home.

I sit with her in the dead
living room at 19 Maple Street
among great voices silent in their sleeves,
and his paintings of the village –

naive, hard-edged, no brush of wonder
or halftone of ambiguity.

When she was young and chestnut-haired
there was a dream that tempted him
and tied him here.
At least, she says with tears, that's how
he told it later in his bitterness –
a twist within the grain I recognise,
remembering that same wounded
wounding thing in his brother
who came back home to stay
and fathered me.

What was it lodged this unforgiving
shrapnel in the bone
of these two brothers?
And home? Did he call Ireland that?
Did he weep for distant deaths
of father, mother, sisters taken
in their bloom? Did he dream back
ghost faces, nights of wind and rain
when he stumbled from *The Patio*?

Toward the end of half a century
he wrote for photographs of places:
Old Bridge, The Weir, The Cottage Walk,
West Gate and Carrickbeg.

4.
Leah drives me through the village,
waving to neighbours, stopping on Main Street
to introduce me to a cop. She's proud of me –
a man from some green valley far away

where seeds of her own destiny were sown.

In Easthampton cemetery
we stand above a bronze plaque
set in sunbleached grass;
under it the ashes
of my father's brother,
the man this woman slept beside
for forty-seven years.

In the explicit blaze of noon
I put my arms around her,
old woman of America
still clinging to the day,
the place, that she's been given,
the fragile courage that she owns.
She kisses me and fumbles for
another menthol tip.

> – *That's it sweetie.*
> *That's all that's left of my Jim.*

His elder son, who owns a penthouse
and a private plane, was too tied up
with flu and real estate
to make the funeral.
Leah, whose people hated Catholics
and Irish most of all, wrote to Carrick
and had him prayed for in the church
where he'd been blessed and named
with candles and with chrism,
with water and the Word.

In Easthampton cemetery
I breathe for him a litany

of distant names of places
only he and I would know.

5.
When cousin Steve has toured me past the pretty homes
he shows me to his buddies at The Country Club.
He stands, back to the bar,
and shouts with pride

> *– Say hello to cousin Mike*
> *from Tipperary Ireland!*

Men in golfing casuals
come up and crowd around.
They shake my hand
because I'm kin to Steve

> *– Tipperary Ireland?*
> *Unbelievable!*

They pay for icecold beers
with credit cards
and while the dark outside
reclaims the trees,
the village and the sea,
they brag about the rounds
they played today,
the deals
they hope to make,
the women
that they long to lay.

Talking of Compassion

A hot day in America.

Near New York city
Melissa Payne, 14, and six
other children wading
off Plum Beach
suddenly step
into deep water.

Remember
Al Turco
and Sal Carbonaro –

we ran out and grabbed
as many as we could,
it was horrible because
we thought they were
just fooling around.

That day, that noon,
I was on Long Island,
an iced drink in my hand,
by a blue pool fluently
talking of compassion
with a woman named Grace Hamor
who lives it out.

Next day I met Melissa Payne
of West 17th Street, Brooklyn,
in a smudged page
of the *Daily News*

dark shroud
of saturated hair,

young limbs stonecold
in sunshine.

A year,
a continent later,
I'd still be feeling
something like guilt
for the death
of a Brooklyn child

I'd be seeing Melissa Payne drown
with an iced drink in my hand
by a blue pool fluently
talking of compassion

I'd be remembering her
and wanting her
to be remembered.

Girl with Fruit and Singers

That day you gave everyone peaches
        songs were sung on all sides
at length and with deep attention
        against taste of juice on the tongue

and peachstones palmed from lips to pockets
        with discretion and best of respect
for the fluent passion emerging
        from the mouth of each singer in turn

who'd come, it seemed, on wind of the word
        that there'd be a songfest there
in a room hushful of reverence
        for the grain in each voice and heart.

The Land and the Song

'Cad a dhéanfaimid feasta gan adhmad?
Tá deireadh na gcoillte ar lár.'

When Jack of the Castle, the last of Kilcash, was buried
A merchant from Carrick bought furniture, flooring and roof,
The great who had lived in the place were ghosts in a poem
Sung under thatch in a tongue that was beggared and doomed.

Only the beaten sang, to remake their story,
To shape a lost self, draw sweetness out of decay;
The strong were never the singers of vanished glory,
Their land was their truth, their poem the power that it gave.

Always this matter of land, its having and holding
Whatever the banners that waved under Slievenamon,
Power lay in fields, however the quarrel was clothed,
This is the daytime truth of what's here and what's gone.

The state has planted a forest of pine and sitka
To yield an acceptable profit in fifty years,
Under the mountain the land and its story's rewritten
By men who own milking parlours and video gear.

The County Council may save the last walls of the castle
For tourists and sentiment tied to some phrase in the song,
Children who chant it at school are serving a piety –
Stammering sounds of lament in a broken tongue.

But out of the fallen woods and the unroofed silence
A dominion endures above unrelenting day –
This place was sung for its trees and a woman's kindness
And the song in itself is whole, and redeems its clay.

The Cup

Before you sleep
take the cup,
toss out the dregs,
turn on the tap

rinse
swill out
and rinse again.

Before you lay it
by to drain

how many mouths
have touched it?

Whose?

How many times?
And when will it
be broken?

For surely the cup
will come
to be broken –

water
lips
and a time for breaking

were implied in the making.

Entrails

Fingers groping
to eviscerate a pheasant
discover the crop
drumtight with acorns,

dreams of oaks
in process of becoming
bird, but for the dark
of circumstance –

the dog at point,
the triggered stagger
in the air
and graceless fall

to earth, into which
are cast the entrails
and the bloodied
acorns.

Out of this may stir
the detonated seed:
intricacy of bird
becoming leaf.

The Story in the Bowl

for Hugh Ryan

Imagine the moment
an acorn settled
in the earth by Slievenamon.
It lay dormant for one winter,
escaped the snout of pig,
the foot of woodkerne, and began
its journey toward my elbow.

In the lush valley of the Suir
cleric, lord and peasant
year by year extemporised
the land's entangled story.
Through circumstantial dark and day
of ten generations
oakwood grew, aloof
from birth-cries,
love-cries,
battle-cries,

until it reached maturity
with Black Tom Butler,
Earl of Ormonde and Elizabeth's
best man in Ireland,
who loved the land
but also loved his queen,
who may have known Shakespeare,
who parleyed with the great O Neill
and took the sword through Munster,
who sent the head of Desmond
to London in a basket.

By Black Tom's order
oak was felled

69

and hauled to Carrick
to build a lightsome manor house
beside the river and the castle
of his ancestors.
His Gaelic poet Eoghan Mac Craith
sang the manor's praises –

Court of the lights of waxen tapers
with sunlit gables and embroidered walls,
where women are courted, gold bestowed,
jewels selected to reward bright sages;
where youths are wooing over silver goblets,
where music and honey are in plenty
and salmon in due season.

Three times married
and a public Protestant
the blind Earl died in bed
at eighty-two, retelling
his Catholic beads,
two years before O Neill
closed his blind eyes in Rome.

Graft into the grain of the oakbeams
another three slow centuries of passing
footsteps through the Long Gallery
while the river Suir by mullioned windows
tided twice through every turning
of the light and dark.

When my great grandfather
was a boatman on the river
the Marquis from Kilkenny
gave the last banquet

in the hall at Carrick
for tenantry and old retainers.

A new tide brought the Irish state
to hold the mansion for the people
and in my time a carpenter, replacing
floor beams of the Long Gallery,
gave to me a block of oak.

Last year I took my slow-grained
prize of time to Bruce MacDonald
of Tasmania and County Waterford
who turned his craft to it
and shaped this bowl
that rests beside my elbow.

It may in time
be someone's heirloom:

what happens next
is stirring in the dark
that waits
behind my shoulder.

The story's open-ended.